Eyelash Wishes

Story and pictures by

LAURA JO STEWART

Story and pictures by

LAURA JO STEWART

*This book is inspired by and dedicated to my children,
and to my little grandson, Everson: Lolli and Pop can't wait to read this to you!*

Printed in the United States of America
First Print, 2021
ISBN 978-0-578-85460-1

LOLLIPOP STORIES

"It's time for bed," said Mom.
"I love you so-o-o-o much, Ryne!"

"I love you too, Mom.
Can I have a kiss and a hug?"
he asked.

"***Of course!***"
she said, as she leaned down
for a hug and kiss goodnight.

As Mom started to get up, she noticed something on Ryne's cheek ...

"Ryne! Guess what you have on your face?" she exclaimed.

"What?" he asked excitedly.

"You have an eyelash on your cheek! That means you get to **make a wish!**" she explained.

Ryne placed the eyelash
on his finger ...
blew really hard ... and
made a wish!

"Yay!" Mom exclaimed.

"You blew it off, so ...
what did you wish for?"

"Did you wish for a pup that you could love and cuddle up?"

"*That's* not my wish," Ryne said with a smile.

"Did you wish for a hot ride
that you can take for a long drive?"

Ryne paused for a moment ...
then announced,
"*That's* not my wish."

"Did you wish for a pool
so you could stay nice and cool?"

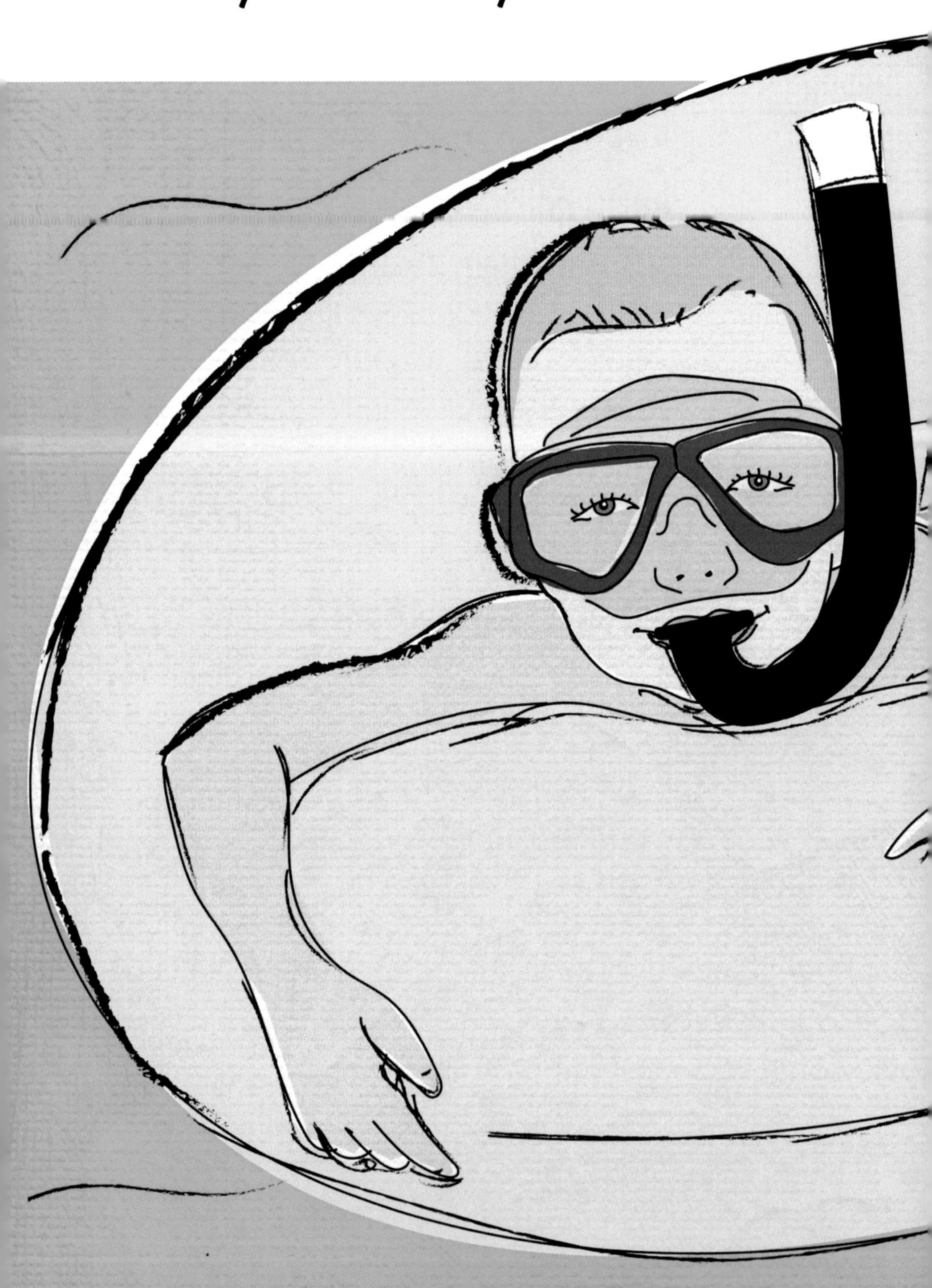

"*That's* not my wish," Ryne said proudly.

Cha-
Ching

“Did you wish for loads of cash?”
she laughed,
all thanks to that **LITTLE** lash?

“***That’s*** not my wish.” he said.

Ring
Ring

"Did you wish for the newest phone
so you could play games,
take pics and even call home?"

"*That's* not my wish,"
Ryne said, once again.

Oh My!

"Did you wish for a room
filled with all sorts of toys?
That'd be a good wish,
if they don't make any noise!"
Mom joked.

"Nope, ***that's*** not my wish either!"
he said with a smile.

Hmm...

Mom was stumped about what Ryne
could have wished for.

"You didn't wish for **a pup**,
or **a car**
or **a pool**
or **cash** ...
not **a phone**,
or **extra toys**
not even another **lash!**

What ***was*** your eyelash wish?"
she asked, one last time.

"I wished for another kiss and a hug!"
said Ryne sweetly.

"Oh Ryne, **OF COURSE**.
That's a wish that will
ALWAYS come true!"
Mom said with a smile.

What would YOU wish for?

A fallen eyelash is a chance to make a wish. If you could wish for anything in the world, what would it be?

ABOUT THE AUTHOR

Born and raised in Des Moines, Iowa, Laura Stewart recognized her love for drawing and painting at an early age. A high school art class assignment to write and illustrate a children's book inspired her dream to make a "real" book. Luckily, she had many wonderful art teachers and professors who helped shape her into the successful graphic design professional she is today. *Eyelash Wishes* is her first published book; she hopes to create more, as her sons Alex and Ryne provide her with daily inspiration.

ISBN 978-0-578-85460-1

9 780578 854601 >

Published by

LOLLIPOP STORIES

Made in the USA
Coppell, TX
10 February 2021